I WON'T BEG FOR
YOUR *Love*

I WON'T BEG FOR YOUR *Love*

R. H. NOTLY

iUniverse, Inc.
Bloomington

I Won't Beg for Your Love

iUniverse books may be ordered through booksellers or by contacting:

iUniverse
1663 Liberty Drive
Bloomington, IN 47403
www.iuniverse.com
1-800-Authors (1-800-288-4677)

ISBN: 978-1-4759-8270-1 (sc)
ISBN: 978-1-4759-8271-8 (ebk)

Library of Congress Control Number: 2013905611

Printed in the United States of America

iUniverse rev. date: 06/14/2013

Chapter One

WHAT THE HELL AM I doing here? These people are getting on my last good nerve. If another person tries to pitch me an idea or ask me to join their organization, I'm going to walk out of here. On Monday, I'll ask my public-relations VP if she was trying to get even with me for, some past infractions. Here comes that woman who gropes me when we dance. I need to get out of here now. Man, I have a headache!

Saying his good-byes to the hostess and some others Omar James headed for the nearest exit.

Serenity Sanders was speaking with some of her clients, Senator James, Mrs. James, and her parents. She looked up and saw a man walking toward an exit and thought. *I wouldn't mind spending some quality time with him.*

Senator James sent a waiter to ask the man to join them. The man didn't walk across the room—he glided, which caused the females in the room with a pulse to react.

Her one and only friend call her the "Laser." Trish gave her the nickname when they were ten years old and away at summer camp. Trish is the sister she never had. According to Trish, she uses her laser look to ward off unwanted attention from men and women. One look makes them stop dead in their tracks.

Just as Omar made it to the exit, a waiter informed him that Senator James wanted to see him. He thanked the waiter and saw the senator waiving at him. He smiled because he was not aware that his parents were in attendance at this function. Upon joining the senator's group he kissed Mrs. James on her left cheek and said, "Hi, gorgeous." He gave the senator a hug and said, "Hi, dad."

The senator introduced Omar to each person in the group. When he got to Serenity's parents, he said, "Mr. and Mrs. Sanders, let me reintroduce you to our son, Omar James. Last—but definitely not least—this lovely lady is none other than Ms. Serenity Sanders."

She took the hand Omar offered and an electric current went straight through her. She shook his hand and could see in his eyes that he also had the same reaction to their hands connecting.

He looked at her and she looked at him. When she was fifteen years old, she learned that boys came from the Planet Sex-Starved—and nothing changed when they became men. That was why she had always given them crazy looks and gotten the nickname from Trish.

Serenity realized that she wasn't looking at this man with the crazy look—and he wasn't looking at her as if she was the appetizer, main course, dessert, and a good drink on legs.

Chapter Two

OMAR JAMES WAS SIX FEET two, well built, with hazel eyes, dimpled cheeks, and brown hair. His smile could put the crankiest of babies to sleep and make grandmothers wish for younger days.

She began to mentally undress him—and then proceed to having some hot, hot sex with him in her head. *Now I can understand why men look at women as if they were the last piece of cheesecake on the dessert tray.* She hoped that while Omar was speaking with her mom and dad, he didn't notice her looking at him. *Damn, the man smells good.*

Omar had seen Serenity at many social events—and looked at her pictures in magazines and on the desk in his father's office—but he could never build up the courage to introduce himself to her. Serenity Sanders was a wet dream for every male between the ages of fifteen and seventy five.

She started modeling and acting when she was fifteen. She graduated from an Ivey League college and started her own company, Sanders Industries, when she was twenty. Now, at twenty-six, she was on the board of directors of several for-profit and not-for-profit corporations. *Can you say over achiever?*

When he was fifteen, his only ambition was running home from school to jerk off in his room. He prayed to the universe that is parents or the housekeeper wouldn't catch him while he was looking at *Playboy.* Standing here next to Serenity made him feel fifteen again. Instead of using his hands to give him release, he wanted to be deep inside of her—and to hear her screaming his name.

Omar and Serenity discussed mutual business acquaintances. Found out they had gone to the same elementary school four years apart—and even had some of the same teachers. He asked her to dance, and she felt good in his arms.

As the evening was coming to an end, Mrs. James invited Serenity and her parents to a fundraiser that she and the senator were having the following weekend for the Sarcoidosis Foundation at their country club.

Serenity told Mrs. James that she would be leaving for Spain in the morning and would be gone for two to three weeks. However, if Mrs. James could give her the specific date and time of the fundraiser, she would mark it as a priority in her PDA and fly back for it.

Mrs. James thanked her and informed her that she didn't have to go out of her way. Serenity told Mrs. James that it was something she wanted to do; flying back would give her the opportunity to relax for the weekend.

Mrs. James again thanked her and shared a smile with her husband and her son.

Serenity asked Mrs. James for her number and immediately texted her private number and her personal assistant's number to Mrs. James. She asked Mrs. James to keep her informed of the details for the fundraiser.

Omar saw an opportunity to give Serenity his personal number and his personal assistant's number, and he asked for her numbers. He told her that he or his PA would keep her informed in case his mother became tied up with her organizations and didn't have the opportunity to call.

They said their good-byes and left.

Chapter Three

OMAR WOKE UP ON SUNDAY morning with a smile on his face and an erection to end all erections. He jerked off while taking a shower and decided to call Serenity to thank her for her kindness to his mother and to wish her a safe trip.

Serenity sounded like she had been woken from a deep sleep.

She said, "Whoever this is, it better be good because you just dragged me from the most wonderful dream."

Omar was not usually flirtatious. He preferred to be introduced to a woman rather than making the introduction himself. He never flirted because it might lead the woman to believe he wanted more than sex.

He said, "I hope you were dreaming about me because I dreamt about you." This surprised him.

Serenity replied, "That is for me to know and you to find out. Good morning, Omar."

He almost fell off the sofa, but he remained calm and said, "Good morning, Serenity. Please accept my apologies for disturbing your dream."

She told him it was all right and asked for the time.

He told her it was ten o'clock.

"Thank you."

"What time is your flight?"

"One o'clock."

"Thanks for supporting my mother's foundation."

"It's something that is important to me too."

He asked if he could escort her to the fundraiser.

She said, "Yes."

He asked if he could call her while she was away, and she said she would like that. He told her to have a safe trip and hung up the phone.

Omar wondered what about this woman made him feel so comfortable to the point where he was flirting with her.

He usually met women through introductions by well-meaning relatives—or they approached him at business functions. Some of the women scared the hell out of him. Some of the questions they asked were off the charts. *Do you love your job? Do you love children? Are your parents alive? How would you feel if your wife decided to stay home after you got married?* One brazen woman went so far as to ask him what his net worth was. With these women, he felt like he was being interviewed for the positions of future husband, sugar daddy, and baby daddy.

Granted, he was already a millionaire and could support his future wife in a lifestyle that would be more than comfortable. He would be damned if he allowed some woman to lasso him into marriage and stay home, shop, be a trophy wife, bump his parents off, and run off to Mexico with the mailman while he is in mourning.

In the near future, he wants a house, 2.5 kids, a dog that can clear a room when it farts, and a wife who he is compatible with in every way. And she better not ask if he loves her. Why the hell would he marry her and subject his future kids to her if she didn't make his heart skip a beat—and it's not from a heart attack.

He will know if she loves him by the way she looks at him, the things she does for him—and to him—and the way she treats him. His parents always told him to judge people based upon their actions instead of their words. *Some people will tell you what they think you want to hear.* His philosophy was to "show me what you got!"

Serenity was smart, beautiful, kind, and appeared to have a good relationship with her parents. He knew that she would never ask what his net worth was because she would have enough sense to go to Forbes.com or buy the magazine to get that information.

Since meeting her, all he could think about was getting her in his bed and keeping her there until he gets her pregnant. Where the hell did that come from? Wanting to make nonstop love with Serenity is different from wanting her to have his kids. But, damn, a little Serenity running around the house would be nice.

Never in his wildest dreams would he have believed that a woman like her would give him the time of day. She dated movie stars and fashion models—if he trusted what he read in the papers and magazines. Was she just being polite because their parents are friends? Did she feel the sparks when they shook hands? It could have been the static electricity from the carpet they were standing on. They weren't standing on carpet—they were standing on wood flooring. He would just call her and take it from there.

Wait a minute—did he just say he was going to call a woman? This was a first; his normal mode of operation was to have his PA call the woman and get him on the line so he could schedule a date for a booty call with the woman. Sometimes his PA scheduled the date and told him when and where to meet the woman.

Damn, Omar Nicolas James III had finally met a woman he would like to have a relationship with. In a month, he had promised to attend a wedding. He might ask her to go with him as his date. Is it okay to take a date to a wedding? The invitation said Omar James III; it didn't mention anything about a guest. Too bad—he was taking a date.

His housekeeper told him that brunch was ready, and he went into the kitchen singing "Finally Found You" by Enrique Iglesias.

Chapter Four

SERENITY SAT UP IN BED wondering if she was still dreaming, Omar James just asked to escort her to a fundraiser, and asked if he could call her while she was traveling. Based on what she heard her parents discussing the night before and what she read in business journals, Omar could be classified has a recluse. He only attends business functions, he endorses worthy causes, and only his inner circle has access to him.

How can a politician's child be reclusive? With both parents in the public arena—and his father's profession and outgoing nature—did Omar have it difficult growing up as a shy child?

From what her parents said—and what the senator had told her over the years—Omar had degrees in forensic science, psychology, and criminal justice. No wonder he was owner and CEO of a global investigative and security company. For all she knew, the man was running a *Men in Black* company, fighting aliens.

He can call her anytime—as long as he's not on the FBI's Ten Most Wanted list; is not a pedophile, rapist, or mentally or physically abusive; doesn't try to control her; and agrees to be her future children's father. *Where did that come from?*

When did she start thinking about men and children? Her mom and Trish would have a field day if they could get a peek in her brain at this moment. She usually thought, *I don't need a man to complicate my life. I can't deal with the possessiveness, jealousy, and crazy shit men put women through*

For all her brains, looks, and money, Trish was always searching for Mr. Right. She kept inviting Serenity to parties so they could meet "eligible" men. No thank you; her hands and her vibrator suit her just fine. Serenity Andrea Sanders—"SAS" to her family—was not ready for any complications.

Not even Trish knew that Serenity was still a virgin. In college, she had a couple of make-out sessions, and she once came close to giving up the goods. Upon second thought, she realized that the guy was not worth it. He would get bragging rights to say that he was her first lover. She would have gotten some sperm and possibly a baby that she was not prepared for.

Her grandmother and her mother always told her to listen to the little voice in her head. It would help her make the right decisions. She was glad that she always listened to that voice. That way, some man looking for his fifteen minutes of fame couldn't sell his story to the tabloids by claiming that he was her first lover.

S ERENITY KNEW SHE WAS PRETTY. She was five feet ten with sun-streaked brown hair that fell almost to the middle of her back. Her golden-brown eyes sometimes gave her a catlike appearance; her face was classically beautiful, and her proportions were on the lean side. Her parents and grandparents had always told her she was pretty. Her parents didn't tell her she was pretty to give her confidence in her appearance. Her grandmother, Mama B, didn't lie or sugarcoat anything.

To keep the boys from sniffing around, Mama B traveled with her from when she was fifteen until she went away to college. Mama B was her chaperone to all the "high-faulting functions," as she called them. Her parents and Mama B had told her that outer beauty fades with time, but inner beauty lasts forever.

At twenty-six, Serenity is a millionaire. When she was in college, she came up with the idea for Sanders Industries. Anything up-and-comers in the fashion, movie, or photography businesses needed, her company could supply at a discount—if they didn't mind that the merchandise was slightly used. She also had her own fashion and perfume line—and a thriving baby clothing and furniture business.

Her parents and Mama B kept her grounded. Her parents still expected her to stack the dishwasher and clean up after herself when she went home for dinner. Mama B called on a regular basis, reminding her to be thankful for her blessings—and to pay it forward.

Serenity had a very good life. She always said that if she didn't have her future children's father in her life by her thirtieth birthday, she would build a house on her land near her parents and Mama B. She would adopt some children. She could work from home; having children wouldn't disrupt her business much. When the children started to need more of her time, she would delegate some of her work responsibilities.

She didn't need a man to validate her intelligence, beauty, or self-worth. She was looking for someone she was compatible with in every way. She wanted someone who would respect her. He should look at her as if she were the only woman in the room. When she is in her sixties, and her body parts are sagging, he needs to look at her with lust in his eyes when he sees her naked. If she's fifty pounds overweight, he will still want to rip her clothes off and have hot, wild sex with her. *Damn, does such a man exist?*

Her father's sister was married to a man who was always telling Aunt Gwen how much he loved her and how beautiful she was. All along, he was sleeping with the divorcée down the block. He fathered a child with her.

No, sir, give me a man who shows me that he loves me with his actions and behavior—and keep me satisfied in the bedroom. Less talk—and a lot of action.

Her future husband and future children's father must be able to tell her children that he loves them unconditionally, and he can't be too busy to play with them. The children must be a priority for both of them. Her parents made time for her and let her know they loved her unconditionally—and they were busy people.

Chapter Six

SERENITY GOT OUT OF BED and started getting ready. Her driver would be there soon to take her to the airport. Trish would be traveling with her for a few days, and she would be in the limo when the driver arrived. Serenity was thankful that she had her own plane and did not have to take a commercial flight.

She remembered the days, even in first class, when she sat next to overbearing businesspeople and in front of screaming children who kicked her seat continuously. Although children could be disruptive, she enjoyed them most of the time. The talkative passengers who asked questions bothered her the most. They made her wonder if they were candidates for a job on one of the TV entertainment shows.

One woman tried to get a lock of hair when she was napping. Serenity's father stepped in, and she became the proud owner of her own aircraft within a month.

When Serenity got in the limo, Trish was on the phone. She was telling someone that he better courier or hand-deliver his child-support check today or she would drop his ass as a client like yesterday's bad news. Patricia Melissa Stow was a woman who nobody wanted to mess with.

Trish owned her own public-relations company and had some of the biggest names in the movie, fashion, sports, and business arenas as clients. And as her initials suggested, she was referred to as PMS when she got angry. Trish was five feet eight and had red curly hair, green eyes, and a sprinkling of freckles across her nose. She was a gorgeous woman with curves in all the right places. She was not fat, but she was not lean like Serenity.

The two women met in first grade when the school bully took Serenity's lunch; Trish punched him in the nose and took it back. The bully tried to get rough with Trish, and both girls tackled him to the ground. One sat on him, and the other used shoelaces to bind his hands and feet. After the incident with the bully, they decided they were sisters, and they became closer than some blood relatives.

When Trish got off the phone, she apologized to Serenity because it would be a working trip for her due to some unforeseen mess with one of her clients. Serenity told her not to worry about it. They proceeded to talked about business, the upcoming fashion week, and Spain.

When they got settled on the plane, Serenity asked Trish what she knew about Omar James.

Trish said, "That man is very private; you two would make a good match."

Serenity smiled and told Trish that she had met Omar at the function she had been forced to attend. Omar's parents and her parents were friends, and Senator and Mrs. James were her godparents. She told Trish about her reaction to him and his phone call.

Trish listened to Serenity while watching her body language and facial expressions.

Serenity never got this animated when she spoke about a man.

Trish sang, "Serenity and Omar, sitting in a tree K-I-S-S-I-N-G. First comes love, then comes marriage, then comes Serenity with a baby carriage."

Serenity looked at Trish, rolled her eyes, and said, "I thought you were turning twenty-seven tomorrow—not seven."

Trish laughed and said, "You have worked with and dated some of the hottest men in the world. I have never seen you look or behave like this."

"Trish, when he touched my hand, I felt an electric charge. It wasn't static electricity because we were standing on wooden floors. He smelled fresh and clean, not overpowered by cologne. When we danced, I wanted to wrap myself around him. All night, all I could think about was getting him naked."

Trish looked at her and said, "Go for it. You never know what will happen until you try."

When they got to Serenity's villa in Madrid on Tuesday morning, they were both tired and jet-lagged. They went to sleep and woke up around four o'clock. They dressed and had dinner on the terrace overlooking the pool, lush gardens, and vineyards. Dinner consisted of crusted salmon in a white-wine sauce, paella, sangria, and flan for dessert.

Serenity gave Trish her birthday gift, a one-of-a-kind Hermes Birkin bag that Trish wanted but had been too frugal to buy for herself. Trish was overjoyed when she received her gift. She thanked Serenity and said, "Now I have to hire a damn bag-guard to protect this bag."

Serenity said, "Don't you mean a bodyguard?"

"No. I don't need guarding, but this bag does."

They both cracked up and then left to meet friends for drinks.

When they returned to the villa, Trish thanked Serenity for a wonderful day and her gift, gave her a hug, and went to bed.

Chapter Seven

SERENITY CHECKED HER PHONE AND realized that it was off. She had several missed calls and messages; two of them were from Omar. She checked her watch and realized it would still be seven o'clock in New York.

Omar picked up after the third ring. She explained that when she traveled, she misplaced her phones or forgot to turn them back on.

He chuckled and said, "I understand. It took me twenty-four hours once before I remembered to turn my phone back on. I guess that is the reason we have personal assistants. If we can't be reached, people call them instead." He asked how her trip was going so far.

She told him about the flight and Trish's birthday. They talked about sports, food, places they had traveled, likes and dislikes, and pet peeves.

Before they knew it, they had been on the phone for two hours. She hated to terminate the call, but she needed to get some sleep before her photo shoot at seven o'clock.

He told her he had enjoyed speaking with her and hoped they could do it again soon.

She told him she had enjoyed it too and would like to hear from him again.

He told her to get some rest; he would call her around eight o'clock that night.

After she hung up, Serenity did her nightly rituals and went to bed. She was exhausted and fell asleep immediately.

Omar went to his home office. He sat on the leather sofa, propped his feet on the coffee table, and leaned back. He started laughing like a fool. He still couldn't believe he had been on the phone with Serenity Sanders—and they had made a connection. It was scary how much they had in common, except for ballet and hockey.

She loves the ballet, and he doesn't; he loves hockey, and she doesn't. As long as she promised not to get their son a tutu, he won't get their daughter hockey gear. Oh hell—he just might get his daughter hockey gear anyway. What rule said hockey is just for boys? He knew, in his heart of hearts, he would marry Serenity Sanders someday.

Chapter Eight

I N THE MORNING, SERENITY AND Trish met in the kitchen. Serenity made a breakfast smoothie, and Trish had an egg-white omelet and a cup of coffee. They ate in silence and went back upstairs to brush their teeth, grab their bags for the day, and headed back downstairs.

In the limo, they smiled at each other, and said good morning. Serenity and Trish were not morning people, but they were forced to function as such because of their professions. When they were together, they allowed each other the space and time to get acclimated to the early hours.

On the drive to the photo shoot, Serenity told Trish about her phone call with Omar and how good it felt to speak with him.

Trish encouraged her to continue the budding relationship to see where it led. She was ecstatic to know that Serenity was finally interested in a man—and he was her equal.

Serenity said, "There is this photographer who is the best in the world. He's booked solid for the next three years—and I snagged him for this photo shoot. His name is Den, and he is Italian."

Trish asked, "What did you say his name was?"

"Den." Trish's eyes started to glow. "He could be your Den."

"Remind me to tell you the story about how I met Den."

The photo shoot was long and exhausting. Working with a new photographer always posed some problem for Serenity, but Den was a charm to work with. He gave directions well; he was calm and relaxed. This resulted in them doing only two or three takes to get the shots needed.

After the photo shoot, they would have gotten back to the villa sooner if Trish and Den hadn't been looking at each other like lovesick puppies and laughing at each other's jokes while they were reviewing the pictures.

When they got in the limo, Trish was smiling and had a goofy look.

Serenity asked her to spill her guts.

Trish said, "Remember the summer when we were fifteen and you started your career? I went to Europe with my parents, and that's when I met Den. He was seventeen, very Italian, and very macho. We disagreed about everything, and he was always around. When I asked my parents why he was following us around, they informed me that they were friends with his parents. Both of his parents had to go out of town on business for the week. His dad offered to take Den with him, but Den wanted to stay with my parents and go sailing.

"I didn't like him. He kept bothering me; I couldn't wait for his parents to return. His parents returned the following week, and we all hung out together. The night before we were to return home, our parents went for a walk on the beach. Den and I stayed on the yacht. We were having another disagreement about something when, out of the blue, Den kissed me and called me 'Bella.' Knowing some Italian, I knew that it meant beautiful. Den told me that he had wanted to kiss me from the first day we met, but he knew that I was a child—and he was afraid of my reaction. I ran to my cabin, locked the door, and called you.

"The next morning, we sailed to France, spent a couple of days there, and flew home. When I got home, Den had left a message for me to call him. My mom said it was okay, so I called him back. When I got him on the phone, he told me that he was not going to apologize for kissing me. He would apologize if he upset me. He asked if we could be friends and if we could call and e-mail each other. I told him yes.

"Over the years, we kept in touch. Whenever I went to Italy or he came to the United States, we would get together as friends."

"So, this is the Den you compare all men to? The one you never stop talking about. No wonder you can't find the right guy for you. You found him when you were fifteen. Now I am glad I asked him to do this photo shoot with me."

"You know what? I think you are right on the money. He is single, and I am single. I am going to pursue a relationship with my first crush and see where it leads."

They both had a siesta when they got back to the villa. They showered, got dressed, and went down for dinner.

Later that evening, Den dropped by to show them the shots he thought were good.

After agreeing on which shots to use in the advertising campaign, Den asked to speak with Trish privately.

Serenity told them to use the study, said good night, and went upstairs.

Chapter Nine

S ERENITY WENT TO HER OFFICE in her bedroom to do some work. She called her PA to let him know that she would be returning to New York for the weekend. He would need to come to Madrid on Thursday and stay until Monday. She needed him to cover for her while she was away.

Just as she was about to wrap it up for the day, her cell phone rang. She smiled when the caller ID showed it was Omar.

He asked about her day, and she asked about his.

He said, "The fundraiser is at eight o'clock. What time should I pick you up?"

"I think 7:30 will be fine."

He asked her what time is her flight getting in on Friday,

"My flight gets in on Friday at midnight."

He thanked her for her generosity in helping his mother's foundation.

She said, "Sarcoidosis is a condition that I am very familiar with because my aunt was diagnosed with the condition fifteen years ago. By reducing stress, daily exercise, healthy eating, and the right combination of vitamins and minerals and getting monitored by her doctors on a regular basis, Aunt Gwen is doing okay."

Omar thanked Serenity for sharing and explained how he understood her passion for the cause. They spoke about causes that are not well known and needed support. They discussed pooling resources to help these causes.

He told her he would like to get to know her better. "Before I met you, I never wanted to call a woman personally. I always had my PA call the woman, and he got me on the phone."

"Ouch! That is cold and disrespectful. Women let you get away with behaving like that?"

"Money let's you get away with a lot."

"That's a copout, and you know it. Everyone deserves respect."

"Point well taken."

"Are you seeing anyone?"

"No."

"I like you a lot. Will you consider being my girlfriend?"

"Are you going to have your PA call me to set up dates?"

"That was cold. I don't think you would allow me to behave like that."

"If you agree not to PA me, then I will agree to be your girlfriend. With our schedules, I don't know how it will work."

"If we want it to work, it will. I am doing a lot of firsts with you. I never had a girlfriend."

"I never had a boyfriend either. Are you going to give me your sweater?"

"Can I pick you up at the airport on Friday instead?"

"I have a driver, but it is nice of you to offer."

"Have breakfast with me on Saturday."

He accepted the invitation and got her address.

She gave it to him and said, "I thought it was your job to locate people?"

"It is. You already believe I am disrespectful. I didn't want to make a bad impression on our first date."

They both laughed and said good night.

Just before the line went dead, Omar said, "I finally found my angel." After hanging up the phone, he started singing "My Girl" by the Temptations.

Chapter Ten

THE NEXT MORNING, WHEN THEY got in the limo, Trish told Serenity that she had been able to resolve her client's issue via phone and e-mail. She was staying until the next day. However, instead of flying back with Serenity, she would be going back with Den. They wanted to start a committed relationship and had a lot to discuss.

Serenity gave her sister a big hug and told her that she was very happy for her. She wished them all the best for a fantastic future.

Trish asked Serenity how it was going with Omar. Serenity told her about their phone conversation.

Trish said, "Serenity has a boyfriend."

Serenity looked at Trish, rolled her eyes, and started to laugh. Serenity would be spending the following week in the Spanish countryside with her longtime photographer. They needed pictures of the locals and the scenery for her perfume TV commercials. She wouldn't see Trish for about a week. They spent Thursday at the spa, did some shopping, and had dinner with friends

Omar called Thursday night. They talked for a couple of hours, and then Serenity went to bed.

On Friday morning, Trish and Serenity went down to breakfast at nine. After breakfast, they left for the airport.

When they got to the airport, Den was already there. They discussed their weekend plans, said their good-byes, and departed.

Serenity got to her apartment after midnight. Omar had left her a text message asking her to let him know when she got in. She texted him back and went to bed.

Chapter Eleven

I N THE MORNING SERENITY, GAVE her New York housekeeper the fright of her life. Mrs. Pen wanted to get an early start on her day, and she decided to start cleaning Serenity's master bedroom.

Serenity had forgotten to let Mrs. Pen know she would be home for the weekend. Mrs. Pen heard water running and singing coming from the bathroom. She knew Serenity wasn't home. Mrs. Pen was prepared to do battle with her cleaning supplies and her mop.

Serenity apologized to Mrs. Pen for scaring her half to death and for not telling her that she would be home. Serenity explained that she would only be home for the weekend and would be leaving on Sunday night.

She asked Mrs. Pen to make breakfast for two because she was expecting company. Her guest would arrive at nine.

Mrs. Pen was baffled because the only company Serenity allowed in her home was her inner circle. Serenity never had visitors.

Chapter Twelve

ON SATURDAY MORNING, OMAR COULDN'T recall if he had slept or not. The only thing on his mind was Serenity—and having breakfast with her. This was another first; he had never been on a breakfast date.

They got along great during their phone conversations, but this would be their first face-to-face, one-on-one interaction. When they were introduced, the parents and others were there. Would they have anything to talk about? Would they still have a connection? What would they do after breakfast?

He was about to leave for Serenity's penthouse when his mother called. She had invited a woman from his father's reelection campaign to the fundraiser because she knew Omar wouldn't have a date.

Toni was always looking at him as if she hadn't been with a man since forever. The woman frightened him; she was always sneaking up on him and blowing him kisses when he visited his father at the office.

He told his mom that he already had a date.

She asked who it was, but he told her she would have to wait and see. He told her to invite his cousin to be Toni's date.

Because he didn't want to have to get a new identity or leave the country permanently. His mother laughed and told him he was being bad. She would take care of the Toni situation.

At 8:30, Omar texted Serenity to find out if she needed him to bring anything. She texted him back: *U*.

At nine o'clock, the security guard called Serenity to announce that Mr. James was there to see her. She told him to send Omar up and went to wait for him by the entry.

The elevator opened into the penthouse entry foyer. Omar looked fine; he was wearing a black T-shirt, black jeans, and Sperry Top-Siders. She had only seen him up close once, and he had been wearing formalwear. *This man looks good no matter what he wears. What does he look like naked?* She wondered if she was drooling.

Omar looked at Serenity. *She looks drop-dead gorgeous.* She was wearing a fitted short T-shirt, cargo pants, no makeup, a ponytail, and Ed Hardy sneakers.

"Welcome to my home." She took his hand.

When they touched, they both felt the electric charge and smiled.

Omar said, "I think this is going to happen every time we touch."

He bent his head to kiss her. At first he just kissed her lips, but then the kiss got deeper. She opened her mouth to give him entry, and he took it. They got to know each other on a different level because of the kiss. He put his tongue in her mouth and kissed her as if they were making love. She responded with little moans and gave him her tongue.

When they came up for air, he kissed her neck, cheeks, and nose. He said, "My angel, if this is breakfast, I can't wait for lunch and dinner."

Serenity loved how it felt to be in Omar's arms. His kisses and his smells do something to me. The man smells fresh and clean.

Chapter Thirteen

T HEY WENT INTO THE KITCHEN, and she introduced
him to Mrs. Pen.

Mrs. Pen looked at Omar and said, "Are you Omar
Jr. and Emily's son?"

He said, "Yes, Mrs. Pen."

She said, "And it is a small world indeed. I have being
Serenity's nanny since they brought her home from the hospital.
She was about two, and you were around six. Your mother and
father had to go out of town and couldn't take you. It broke their
hearts to leave you because they took you everywhere with
them. Mr. and Mrs. Sanders told them that we would be happy
to take care of you for the weekend. That weekend, Serenity
followed you around on her wobbly little legs. You were very
patient with her, and you watched out for her. I think you have
turned into a very handsome young man."

He gave her his dimpled smile and said, "Thank you."

Mrs. Pen served omelets with spinach, mushrooms, and
red, green, and yellow peppers; homemade croissants; fresh
orange juice; coffee; and tea.

When Mrs. Pen left, Omar looked at Serenity and said, "I am really your first boyfriend?"

She laughed and said, "That doesn't count."

To take their minds off the obvious sexual desire for each other, they ate and talked about their teachers in elementary school

After breakfast, Omar asked Serenity what she wanted to do before the fundraiser.

"I'm tired and want to hang out at home with you—if that's okay."

"That is more than fine with me."

Chapter Fourteen

S HE TOOK HIM INTO HER game room. When he saw the room, Omar wanted to ask Serenity to marry him immediately.

The woman had a sixty-inch, state-of-the-art flat-screen TV, arcade-quality games, and a pool table. To top it off, she showed him the theater room with seats for ten people. She smiled and told him that she also had a bowling alley and a swimming pool on the first floor.

Since she was always in the public eye, she preferred to say in and entertain herself at home. Due to their schedules, Trish was not always available to hang with her.

Omar told Serenity that she could call him or come over to his place whenever she wanted company because he had a game room similar to hers—minus the movie theater, bowling alley, and swimming pool. He traveled a lot for his job. When he was home, he preferred to stay in.

Serenity smiled and said, "I fully understand—and I prefer to be around the people who are closest to me."

Omar gave her a hug and said, "Me too."

The second time they kissed, it was more intense than the first. Omar plundered her mouth with his tongue while pushing his hips into hers. He caressed her breasts. Her nipples hardened, and the wetness between her legs was unlike anything she had ever felt. She could feel Omar's erection and knew that he wanted her as much as she wanted him. She hesitated a moment, and he looked in her eyes.

He could tell she was scared. Her released her, kissed the corners of her mouth, and said, "How good are you at pool?"

"Very good. My dad taught me how to play. During his college days, he played in pool tournaments." She told him to give her about half hour to make some phone calls and then he could show her how good he was.

He looked her in the eyes and said, "Angel, I am better than good." The look he gave her told her he wasn't talking about pool.

To give her some privacy, he went to the theater to look around, but she told him he could stay.

She called her mom to let her know that she had gotten back safely. She called her grandmother, and they talked for a while. Mama B cracked her up with stories about her friends. She gave Mama B kisses over the phone, told her she loved her, and asked to speak with her Pop-Pop. They spoke for a while; she told him she loved him and hung up.

She called Trish. Her best friend sounded like a woman in love. Trish told her that she was in bed with Den and was fully sated. Serenity said she was with Omar and was having fun. They both laughed and said they would speak again in a couple of days.

Omar and Serenity played games for kisses. They watched movies, had lunch, and slept in each other's arms on the sofa in the den. Around four o'clock, Omar told her he would come back to get her and left to get ready for the fundraiser.

On the way home, Omar went over the day's events in his head. It was the best time he had ever spent with a woman without having sex. *Wait a minute—this is the only time I have spent with a woman without having sex. Another first.*

The day was romantic, fun, and relaxing. He looked forward to many more days like this one with her.

Serenity took a relaxing bath and wondered if being with Omar would always be like today. She couldn't remember having so much fun with anyone—not even Trish. She had come close to making love with Omar.

Tonight when he takes me home, we will make love! Darn. I don't want Mrs. Pen to walk in on us.

She would have to explain to Mrs. Pen that Omar is now her boyfriend—and she would need some private time with him. She would be locking the doors to her bedroom suite when she was home. Tonight they could go to his place.

After she got out of the tub, there was a text from Omar asking her to call him.

When he answered the phone, he said, "I had a fantastic day with you today. I would like to wake up with you by my side tomorrow morning. Pack an overnight bag so you can spend the night with me. If you feel like I am moving too fast, please let me know."

"Right now, you are moving at the perfect speed. I'll pack my overnight bag."

Chapter Fifteen

A T SEVEN O'CLOCK, SERENITY CALLED the security
desk and told the guard to send Omar up when he
arrived.

Omar got off the elevator just as Serenity was coming
toward the foyer. She was dressed in a deep purple silk dress
with a high jeweled neckline; the dress fell above her knees
and hugged her slender curves to perfection. She wore purple
Manolo Blahniks with jewel straps, and she had a matching
clutch. She wore amethyst earrings, a ring, and a bracelet.

Omar thought Serenity looked demure and beautiful. When
she turned around to pick up her cell phone from the console,
he saw the back of the dress. He immediately changed his mind.
There was nothing demure about this dress. The dress was cut
very low in back; the jewels from the neckline ran down the
sides and ended in a V. This dress was seductive without being
vulgar.

Omar wore a midnight-blue suit, white cotton shirt, and a
light purple necktie with amethyst cuff links; they both laughed
at how well they were coordinated.

Serenity asked Omar where he parked. He told her that his driver was waiting out front. She told him to have the driver go to the parking garage under the building to prevent them from being bothered when they exited the building.

In the elevator, Omar wondered if Serenity was wearing any underwear beneath her dress. Thank goodness the elevator ride was short—because he was tempted to find out.

Chapter Sixteen

O N THE RIDE TO HIS parent's country club in Westchester County, Omar told Serenity that he liked how she was close to her parents. He asked about her fondest childhood memories, and she told him about her summer vacations driving across the country with her parents, grandparents, and Trish.

From the time they were seven, she and Trish would spend two weeks at summer camp and three to four weeks traveling the country with her family. Her dad told them they were getting an interactive history lesson.

Omar said, "How many states have you visited?"

"All fifty."

"Which is your favorite?"

"New York."

"Although I have only visited twenty-five states, New York is my favorite too."

"Why New York?"

"I have homes in different states and other countries, but New York is where my roots are."

"Nicely put."

Serenity asked Omar what it was like growing up as the son of a politician.

He told her about his wonderful childhood. When he was a child, he had the opportunity to go to work with his dad in the nation's capital. This allowed him to go places that others only dreamed about. He got to meet presidents, senators, and congressional leaders. He told her how he was always quiet and shy, but his parents allowed him to be himself. He didn't grow out of his shyness, and his job allowed him to maintain a certain amount of anonymity. Outside of his inner circle, she was the first female under the age of fifty-five who made him feel comfortable—and sex wasn't involved. Being with her relaxed him.

Serenity let him know how her job forced her to be a public person, but she was very introverted. Other than her inner circle, he was the only person she felt comfortable with.

He told her he was glad they had found each other, and gave her a kiss on her forehead.

Chapter Seventeen

WHEN THEY WALKED INTO THE reception room at 8:45, almost everyone was there. The group consisted of politicians, doctors, lawyers, a retired actress who was married to one of the doctors; many others were also in attendance.

All eyes were on Omar and Serenity. Emily James came over, gave them big hugs, and thanked Serenity for coming. She escorted them to a group that Serenity's parents and the senator were speaking with. After hugs from her parents and the senator, they were introduced to the others in the group.

Her parents and Emily James looked surprised to see them together. The senator was not surprised; he introduced them so they could get to know each other. He had always thought they would make a good match. He would be retiring soon and wanted grandchildren.

Omar and Serenity danced with each other and mingled with the other guests. He kept her at his side the entire time. At one point, she whispered her thanks for not leaving her side. When she attended functions, she was usually asked strange questions—and her space was invaded. That was the reason she always took her parents, Trish, or her grandparents.

When Serenity went to the ladies' room, Omar's cousin stopped him and asked. "What is the CEO and president of the geek club doing with a woman like Serenity?" Rob slapped Omar's shoulder. "You know that she is out of your class, right?"

Omar laughed and said, "Sometimes geeks get a break and end up with the homecoming queen."

When she was returning from the ladies' room, Toni approached her and said, "You are way prettier in person."

Serenity thanked the woman, and Omar was immediately at Serenity's side.

He told Toni that Serenity was his girlfriend.

Toni told him they looked good together and walked away.

After Toni left, Serenity whispered, "The way that woman looked at me is scary."

Omar hugged her and whispered, "I think she is a stalker-in-training. She scares me too." He took Serenity aside and explained everything about Toni.

Serenity couldn't hide her laughter, and both of them started laughing.

Everyone in attendance made large donations to the Sarcoidosis Foundation. Emily James declared the night a success, and she credited Serenity for the outcome.

The majority of the group started leaving around midnight.

Serenity and Omar spoke with both sets of parents for a while longer. Her parents suggested that they stay over and leave early in the morning. Serenity reminded them that she had a flight back to Spain and would rather sleep in than get up early. She said she would give them a call before leaving for Spain.

She kissed her parents, hugged the senator and Mrs. James, and left with Omar.

Chapter Eighteen

WHEN THE CHILDREN LEFT, DOROTHY Sanders said, "Our children look as if they are a couple. Has Omar said anything to you?"

Emily agreed and said that Omar had only told her he was bringing a date—and that was all.

Omar's father looked at the others and said, "I introduced them at that function because I knew they would make a good match. I will be ready for grandchildren in a few years, and that son of mine needed a push in the right direction."

Will Sanders looked at Omar Jr. and said, "You know that Serenity is normally a shy girl and doesn't like to mingle. That is why we—or her friend Trish—always attend social functions with her. Based on what we saw tonight, she will no longer need our services."

Emily explained how Omar had always been very shy and not very social. "Looking at them tonight, you would never have known that the boy was a recluse. When he was ten, he told us he didn't like people because they invaded his space. Only his family is allowed to invade his space."

Omar Jr. laughed and said, "I guess we will be having an addition to both families soon."

Both sets of parents hugged good night and went to their cars.

Chapter Nineteen

O**N THE RETURN TRIP TO** the city, Omar told Serenity that, ever since he had first seen her in that dress, he wanted to know if she was wearing underwear.

She asked what was stopping him from finding out. He unhooked the clasp at the back of her neck, and the dress fell to her waist, revealing her naked breasts.

After admiring them for a while, he took a nipple in his mouth and suckled while playing with the other breast.

She started moaning while leaning into his mouth.

He lifted Serenity onto his lap, and she began to gyrate on his erection.

She moved her hand down to Omar's crotch, unzipped his pants, reached in, and released his engorged penis. While he suckled and played with her breast, she massaged and stroked his penis.

She continued to gyrate on Omar's penis while stroking him.

He continued to suckle, massage, and pull on her breast and nipples. Omar began to move his hips while she continued her movements on his penis. He moved to her other breast and said, "You are very responsive." He gave her other breast the same attention, and it drove her wild.

She felt her panties getting soaked and wanted to feel more. Their moaning got louder as the sensations they were feeling got stronger.

A block before they got to Omar's apartment building, Serenity threw her head back and climaxed. Omar covered her mouth with his to stifle her screams.

A few seconds later, Omar found his release, and she kissed him to stifle his moans. He pulled her to him, looked in her eyes, and said, "Another first. You are the first person to make me climax in a limo."

She said, "This is a first for me too. I have never made love in a limo."

He hooked her dress back up, cleaned himself off with his handkerchief, and zipped up his pants. When the limo stopped, he looked at her and said, "Let's go discover some more firsts."

When they entered Omar's building from the underground garage, Serenity saw six black Mercedes-Benz SUVs.

"Are you partial to black SUVs?"

"They are for business. My personal cars are parked on the other side of the garage."

"I have a driver's license, but I don't see the need to have a car in the city. I only drive when I visit my parents."

All discussions about cars were forgotten when they got to the elevator. By the time they got off the elevator, they were both partially nude and leaving a trail of clothes on the way to his bedroom. They undressed each other and admired what they had uncovered.

Looking at his six-pack, Serenity could tell that Omar worked out. When she saw his erection, she wondered if she would be able to take all of what he would be giving her.

Omar looked at Serenity and told her she was his beautiful angel. He wondered how he had gotten so lucky because she was way out of his class—and he was about to make love to her.

She was shaking. He took her in his arms and told her not to be nervous. He would take it slow and gentle.

She told him she had made out with a couple of boys in college, but she had never allowed any of them to have sex with her.

He hugged her tighter and said, "You mean I would be your first?"

"Yes."

"Why me?"

"It just feels right. You make me feel safe and secure."

He held her tightly and said, "I have never had sex with a virgin. This is another first for both of us." Omar could sense that Serenity was still nervous. "We'll just explore each other for now."

She trusted him, and he helped her to relax by massaging her scalp, neck, and shoulders.

They kissed and explored each other.

Omar said, "Show me how you pleasure yourself."

She was surprised by his statement.

He said, "Don't be embarrassed, angel. I pleasure myself. If you have never pleasured yourself, I will show you how to do it—and we will do it together. It will make you less nervous and more relaxed."

She started to fondle her breasts and pull on her nipples. She moved her other hand down and start fondling the sensitive spot between her legs. She looked up and saw that Omar was fondling his penis while looking at her. The look in his eyes was pure lust.

Watching Omar fondle himself turned her on. She could feel herself getting wetter and wetter. *This is better than when I am alone.*

Still looking into Omar's eyes, she opened her legs and put one of her fingers into her vagina. She started pumping it in and out while massaging her sensitive bud with her thumb.

He looked down; what she was doing drove him wild. They reached their peaks seconds apart and fell on the bed sated.

Omar got up and went into the bathroom. Serenity heard the shower running. He came back in the bedroom and told her to hold on. He left the room and returned with two chopsticks. He asked her to scoot down on the bed; he proceeded to put her hair on top of her head and secured it with the chopsticks.

He picked her up, took her into the bathroom, and stepped in the shower with her. He kissed her cheeks and moved to her lips, sucking and kissing them. He sucked on the pulse beating at her neck, and it drove her wild. He moved down to her breasts and took one in his mouth while kneading and pulling on the nipple of the other. He switched breasts and gave her other breast the same treatment. He kept moving down; when he got to her navel, he stuck his tongue inside and twirled it around.

Serenity felt like she was crawling out of her skin. She had never felt anything like this before.

Omar kept moving down and showering her with kisses and licks until he got down to her lower lips. He said, "Open your legs for me."

By this time, her body was on fire. She had no choice but to do what he asked.

He took her into his mouth and alternated between sucking her sensitive bud and pushing his tongue inside her. He put her legs over his shoulders and ate her like she was his last meal. She had never experienced anything like what he was doing to her, and it was driving her insane. She dug her hands in his hair and held on for dear life; her world was spinning out of control. She came with such force that he had to hold her up while he continued to suck every last drop of her juices.

Omar washed both of them with body wash, wrapped them in the largest bath sheet Serenity had ever seen, and took her back to bed. He showered her with kisses again and used his thumb to play with her sensitive bud. He inserted two fingers inside her and rotated them; he pulled them out and put them back in. His action with his fingers mimicked what his penis would do. Serenity bent at the waist and rose off the bed, moaning and gyrating.

He continues to do this until she was on the verges of another climax. He entered her very slowly, inch by inch. When he reached the barrier of her hymen, he pushed his tongue deep into her mouth while doing the same with his penis at the other end of her body.

When he felt her stiffen, he stopped pushing his penis into her—but he kept kissing her. When she started to rotate her hips, he knew it was his sign to start moving his penis inside of her again. He continued with steady, gentle strokes until she begged him for release—and then he gave it to both of them.

After they could breathe again, Omar hugged her and asked if she was hurting.

"No. I want to see stars again."

"We will both see stars many more times before you leave for Spain, but now you need to rest."

He was true to his words. Omar and Serenity made love several times during the early morning into daylight—and they both saw stars. They fell asleep clinging to each other, and it felt good for both of them.

Chapter Twenty

SERENITY WOKE UP DISORIENTED, BUT she remembered she was in Omar's bedroom. She reached over to say good morning, but Omar was not in bed.

She went into the master bathroom, did her morning rituals, put on his bathrobe, and went looking for him. She followed the smell of coffee and found him in the kitchen. He was making French toast and peeling oranges for the juicer. She asked if he needed any help, but he said he was good.

She said, "You aren't just good—you are fantastic."

He looked at her and gave her a shy smile. *That face and those dimples—the man should come with a warning sign.*

Breakfast was delicious. Serenity asked when he learned to cook. He told her that his mother couldn't cook; he remembered her burning water on several occasions. The housekeeper and his father taught him how to cook. They didn't want him to starve when he went away to college

"Did you live on campus when you were in college?"

"A buddy and I shared an apartment off campus."

The only thing I am good at in the kitchen is making fresh juice, omelets, or reservations."

"Cooking is something you love to do or you don't. My mother told my father that he didn't marry her for her cooking skills; therefore he should appreciate whatever she put on the table. He asked her to please stay out of the kitchen."

They were comfortable talking with each other, discussing the pitfalls of constant travel.

She had her future planned out, and it didn't include traveling all over the world. "I haven't shared this with anyone. A year ago, I decided I am going to retire from modeling and acting when I turn twenty-eight. I'm going to focus on my business and designing. If I am not married or have a life partner by the time I am thirty, I will adopt two children, move to the suburbs, raise my children, and run my businesses and design studio from my home."

Omar was very impressed with Serenity's plans. He also planned to stop globetrotting as soon as he found a wife and started a family because he wanted to be a caring, attentive husband and a hands-on father—just like his own father. He said, "What qualities do you want in a husband or life partner?"

"I am very straightforward, and I treasure honesty. He must have trust, friendship, fidelity, and his deeds and actions should say more than his words because actions speak louder than words. My turnoffs are men who behave like cavemen and don't give their partners breathing room. Jealousy is a big turnoff. I have to work with men all the time. If the man in my life is not secure enough to know that I wouldn't degrade myself—or him—by cheating or having an affair, then he is not the right man for me. I've had enough drama in my career; I don't need it in my personal life."

Chapter Twenty-One

OMAR ASKED, "DO YOU READ minds? Except for the caveman thing, those are the exact qualities I need in a wife. What about love?"

Serenity said she would know if her man loves her by how he treats her, reacts to her, the look in his eyes, and the tone he uses when he speaks with her. She didn't need to hear "I love you" daily because it becomes dated and unbelievable. She needs to hear it when it is not expected. People say "I love you" without meaning it. She needs her man to show her that he loves her.

Omar looked at her and said, "For someone so young, you are very insightful and grounded."

"The credit should go to my parents and grandparents."

"What does your schedule look like the last weekend of June? I've been invited to my college roommate's wedding that weekend, and I'd like you to go with me."

"As far as I know, my calendar is clear from June 10 to July 7. For the first time in eleven years, I am going to take a break and exhale."

She would be his date if he informed the bride and groom that she would be attending—and asked them not to tell anyone because she didn't want to overshadow the bride. They also would have to sit in the back of the church or wherever the wedding ceremony was been held.

He looked at her and said, "You are serious—aren't you?"

"Yes. I love my life, but it sucks at times like this. Through no fault of my own, other people's lives get disrupted by my presence. Do you still want to get involved with me?"

"Wild horses couldn't drag me away. If you are on board, I would like to pursue a relationship with you and see where it leads."

She hesitated, looked at him, and said that she was on board.

He wondered. Why the hesitation?

She said, "We need to talk about the unprotected sex we had last night and this morning. An unplanned pregnancy has no place in my life at this point in time. Are you in the habit of having unprotected sex?"

"Last night was the first time in my life I ever had unprotected sex."

"When I return from Spain, I will ask my doctor to put me on a birth-control plan. I know we will be having more sex in the future."

He looked at her lustfully, smiled, and said, "Every chance we get."

She asked him to go to the drugstore to get a morning-after pill. If she went to the store, it would be in the tabloids and on *Entertainment Tonight* before she leaves the store.

He said, "I will take care of it." He left the room to phone someone. When he returned, he told her that his doctor would be over in twenty minutes to give her a shot.

She gave him a questioning look, but he informed her that he employed people in a variety of professions. She thanked him and left to take a shower.

The doctor arrived, gave her the shot, and told her to rest for the remainder of the day. She told him that she would be on an international flight in about four hours. He told her to rest on the plane. She thanked the doctor, and Omar walked him to the elevator.

Chapter Twenty-Two

THEY RELAXED ON OMAR'S LARGE leather sofa in his family room, eating grapes and drinking sparkling water. When she went in the bedroom to get her things, Omar asked her to leave the outfit she wore to the fundraiser in his closet because he wanted to stay connected to her

On the drive to her apartment, he asked if she was going to tell her parents and Trish that they were a couple.

She asked if it was important to him that others knew about their relationship status, and He said, "Yes".

She promised to tell her parents, her grandparents, and Trish.

He told her that he would let his parents know; this would stop his mother from trying to find him a woman. He explained how he was pretty sure his father was playing matchmaker when he introduced them.

She said, "Your father would do that?"

"Yes. My father is as subtle as a bull in a china shop."

Serenity then dropped a bomb on Omar. "All these years when your dad would call me to see how I was doing and gave me updates about you, I thought he was being a good godparent and a proud father. Don't tell me he was playing matchmaker."

He was thankful to be in the limo because he would have wrecked the car if he was driving. He looked at her and said, "My father is your godfather?"

"And your mother is my godmother."

"What does that make us?"

She looked at him and said, "Lovers."

She called her parents and, after recapping the fundraiser with her mom, she asked her to have her dad pick up the other phone because she had something to tell them. When her dad picked up the phone, she told them about Omar. She let her mom know that the two mothers should not start planning a wedding or do anything else to embarrass their children.

Her mother chuckled and said, "I wouldn't do anything like that."

Serenity and her dad both said, "Yes, you would."

They chatted some more and then disconnected the call.

Omar called his parents, and his father answered the phone. They talked for a while, and he asked his father to get his mother on the line because he needed to speak with them together. When his mother got to the phone, they spoke for a while. He told them about Serenity and how he expected them to respect their privacy and not call a news conference as soon as he got off the phone.

Omar asked them why they hadn't told him that Serenity was their goddaughter.

His father said, "Didn't you get a clue that she was important to us when you saw all the pictures of her in my office—and they weren't from a magazine?"

Omar let that one go. He chatted with his parents some more; before he disconnected the call, they both told him to give Serenity a kiss for them. He said he would and ended the call.

Omar looked at Serenity and smiled. He leaned over and kissed her on both cheeks and said, "That's from my parents."

He took her to her apartment to get her bags, and they left for the airport.

On her plane, she sat on his lap, kissing and making out. When her pilot announced that they were ready for takeoff, they shared one last passionate kiss before Omar left the plane.

He stood on the tarmac and watched the plane disappear into the clouds. For the first time in his life, he knew what loneliness felt like. *Is this how it's going to feel whenever we have to part? How did I allow her to sneak past my defenses and steal my heart so quickly?*

Omar knew his heart was on that plane bound for Madrid. He felt heart palpitations—and hoped it wasn't something he had eaten or a damn heart attack.

Chapter Twenty-Three

SERENITY SLEPT FOR THE MAJORITY of the flight. When she got to the villa, she had a cup of tea, took a shower, and put on one of Omar's T-shirts. He had given her seven of his T-shirts to sleep in—one for each night—and they all had that special Omar scent that made her want to cuddle. She laughed and knew they both had it bad—whatever "it" was.

She texted him to let him know she had arrived safely, and that she had enjoyed the wonderful time with him on Saturday and Sunday. She would speak with him later to let him know her schedule for the next couple of weeks.

She texted her parents and Mama B, read her e-mails, and called her PA at the guest house to let him know that she need him to stay in Spain for the next week or two. Before she put the phone down, she could have sworn she heard him say, "Yeah. That's what I'm talking about."

Her PA had been recommended by her manager; although he was a recent college graduate with minimal experience, he was doing a great job. She called Trish and left a message. When she was finished it was about five o'clock in the morning. She put her phone on silent and went to bed to get a couple of hours of sleep. The limo would be picking her up at nine.

Omar read Serenity's text and replied that he was glad to hear that all was well—and he had enjoyed Saturday and Sunday as well.

Saturday and Sunday had been the most perfect days he had ever spent with anyone. And he was looking forward to her call the next day. He started thinking about the two days they had spent together.

She was unlike any woman he had spent time with. She was smart, talented, outspoken, she dealt with him as an equal—and not like some god because he had money. She had her own money; his money didn't impress her. She told him what she would accept and what she wouldn't accept.

He had come close to telling her that a pregnancy would make him a happy man, but he backed off when she said a child was not part of her plan for two years. She was twenty-six, and he was thirty; they had time. He could wait a couple of years to start a family. He wondered if she would be open to marriage in the meantime because having her in his bed felt great.

Omar started thinking realistically about their careers. How would living in different countries for weeks or months at a time affect a marriage? He decided to try working on being a couple for now.

Just as he was about to turn in for the night, he received a frantic call from one of his oldest clients. Hector Miguel was normally a calm, rational man. However, he was calling from his home in Mexico because his twenty-five-year-old son was missing. Hector didn't know if Pedro had been kidnapped or if he ran off with his pregnant girlfriend. Hector didn't trust the police in his country and did not want any publicity. He needed Omar's help.

Omar told Hector to e-mail or fax him all the details about Pedro and the girlfriend. He would have his VP of operations in his Mexico office get on the case immediately. Omar contacted his office in Mexico and updated Bernie on their new case. Omar didn't need to remind him that the case was a priority.

Chapter Twenty-Four

AFTER MEETING WITH HER CREW to finalize the schedules for the coming week, Serenity called Omar. He said, "Hello, my angel."

She laughed and asked how he was doing

He told her he missed her.

She told him that she missed him also.

They talked about the previous weekend and how exciting and comfortable being with each other felt. They discussed their schedules and upcoming travel plans.

She told him that she had received e-mails from her studio, her manager, and Trish. The release date for her latest film had been moved up. She would start a promotional tour for the American release of the film on June 1.

He asked about her plan to take some time off to exhale, and she said that it had to be postponed. The film's premiere would be the next Saturday. He would be out of the country and couldn't be with her. For the remainder of June, she would have to travel to England, Italy, France, Spain, and Germany to promote the film.

He asked if she would be able to get away for the wedding.

Serenity said she would, but she sounded sad, lonely, and exhausted.

Omar had to travel to Dubai, Turkey, and Korea from July until September. He wanted to do something for her, and he asked what hotel she was staying in. She told him that she was staying at her home in Madrid.

They spoke for another couple of hours, and she tried to convince him that they should put their budding relationship on hold until their schedules had them in the same country for more than a week at a time. He convinced her not to give up on them. They could find a way to make it work.

Omar asked Serenity about her schedule for the week.

Serenity's group would be traveling around Madrid and the countryside for four to six hours per day taking pictures for her perfume advertising campaign. It would feel like a vacation to her, and she was going to enjoy it.

He told her he would be sending her a surprise. It would be waiting for her when she got home from work the next day.

She asked him to tell her about the surprise, but he wouldn't. He encouraged her to get some rest and they would speak again the next day. She thanked him for listening to her venting about her crazy life. He informed her that he would always be there for her, and she could vent to him anytime.

She said, "Sleep well," and disconnected the call.

When Omar got off the phone, he went to work getting her location in Madrid. He called his pilot to let him know they were leaving for Madrid at eleven o'clock in the morning.

Chapter Twenty-Five

FOR FIRST TIME IN HER life, Serenity cried in her pillow and wished she had a different life. She composed herself long enough to wonder if having a romantic relationship at this point in her life was worth the baggage it brought with it.

She had made a conscious effort not to get involved romantically with anyone because she had seen what this life could do to a romance. She didn't want to be divorced and remarried six times before she was thirty-five. Now this man had come along and made her world spin out of control. Whenever she saw him, spoke with him, or got a text message from him, she fell in love with him more and more.

That man is slick. He gave me those damn T-shirts to sleep in, and they all have his sexy smell. Now all I can smell is Omar.

Her heart was telling her to chuck it all, call the studio, her manager, her agent, Trish, her parents, and Mama B to tell them she was retiring from acting and modeling to concentrate on running Sanders Industries. She would ask Omar to run off with her to Bali and leave the world behind. Her head took over and reminded her of her responsibilities to the studio, the modeling agency, her manager, her agent, and Trish.

Serenity asked herself how she could have allowed her life to become so complicated in two short weeks. She lived a life without complication; she didn't like drama. She did what needed to be done without thinking about missing anyone—but a man came into her life and turned it upside down. Men were nothing but trouble, and she had willingly invited trouble into her life.

Ever since she was fifteen, she knew she could not be like other girls. She had chosen this life because it is what she wanted. Her parents supported her decision and had helped her along the way. They provided her with the emotional support she needed to survive in the business. Along with her parents and grandparents, Trish was always there when she needed a shoulder to cry on or someone to laugh with. Now she was getting that same support from Omar—something she had never expected from anyone outside of her inner circle.

She was facing a bigger dilemma than their schedules. She was not ready to make their relationship public. When the media and the paparazzi found out that she was in a relationship, they would hound them to death. She was not ready to see her personal life spread across the front page of every tabloid in the world. Tears ran down her cheeks. She closed her eyes and fell asleep while thinking about Omar.

Chapter Twenty-Six

SERENITY WOKE UP THINKING ABOUT Omar and kept wondering what her surprise was. She and the crew had a very successful day taking pictures around Madrid. Around four o'clock, they called it a day. She went back to the villa, thinking about her surprise.

She asked her housekeeper if a package had been delivered for her, but Rosa said no. Serenity thanked her and went upstairs to take a shower. She was in her office when Rosa called her on the intercom to inform her that she had a visitor in the study. She told Rosa that she would be down in a minute.

Omar was looking out the window with his back to the door. When Serenity opened the door to her study, she knew immediately that her visitor was Omar. He was her surprise. She walked quietly up to him, hugged him around his waist, and said, "This is the kind of surprise I love."

He turned around, picked her up, and kissed her all over her face and neck. And then he ravished her mouth with his. When they came up for air, he walked her to the sofa and sat down with her in his arms.

She asked how he had found her. He smiled and told her that, in his business, he could find anyone—anywhere. She told him she was happy he came and asked how long he could stay.

He asked, "How long do you want me to stay?"

"Forever."

"You can count on that."

They basked in the comfort of each other's arms.

Serenity asked Omar what he did for a living.

He said, "Officially I am a security and investigative expert with offices worldwide."

"And unofficially?"

"You would need a high-level security clearance for me to discuss anything with you. And even then, it would have to be on a need-to-know basis."

She laughed and said, "I knew it. You are running the *Men in Black* organization!"

Omar laughed and said, "Take me to your bedroom, and let us play among the sheets."

On the way up to her bedroom Serenity reminded Omar that she was not on birth control—and she didn't keep condoms in the house. The protection was on him; if he didn't have any, all they would be doing was making out.

He looked crestfallen. He said he had forgotten to bring protection and would get some tomorrow. Tonight, he would show her how they could pleasure each other with their hands and mouths.

She said, "Do you always have a backup plan for everything?"

"Yes—except when it comes to you. I have no backup plan or exit strategy—and it scares me."

She gave him a kiss on his chest, hugged him tightly, and didn't say anything.

Chapter Twenty-Seven

WHEN THEY GOT TO HER bedroom, his phone rang. He looked at it and said, "I should answer this."

She pointed to her office and told him he would have privacy in there.

He answered the phone very abruptly. "Bernie, this better be an emergency for you to be calling me on my private number."

Bernie told Omar that the office in Madrid was trying to locate him. They were afraid to call him on his personal line because Omar had told them if they didn't stop calling his personal line, he would bury them so deep in paperwork they would never see the light of day again.

Omar laughed and told Bernie that he would call the Madrid office. He asked Bernie if he had found Pedro.

Bernie said yes; the report had just been sent to Omar. Pedro ran off to San Diego to marry his girlfriend because he couldn't take the family drama anymore. Pedro and his girlfriend were American citizens and had no problem crossing the border. Hector was informed of his son's whereabouts, and father and son promised to contact each other.

Omar told Bernie he liked how Pedro had taken charge of his life and didn't allow his family and his new wife's family to dictate his faith.

Bernie agreed, and they terminated the call.

While he was on the phone, Serenity asked Rosa's husband to bring Omar's bags upstairs. She told Omar's security person and driver that they could stay in the three-bedroom suite behind the game room. It had access to the main house through the game room and a private entrance from the veranda. They could have their meals with her PA, Rosa, and Juan.

Chapter Twenty-Eight

W HEN OMAR RETURNED TO THE bedroom, his clothes were hanging in a spare closet in Serenity's bedroom, a bath had been drawn for him. The last time he remembered taking a bath was when he was seven. If his woman drew him a bath, he would take a bath. If she joined him in the bathtub, it would be even better. He loved it that Serenity took charge of the accommodations for his men and was taking care of him.

After three minutes, Omar realized why his mother always said she was going to take a bath when he and his father got on her nerves. The bath was so relaxing! He closed his eyes. When he felt the water move, he opened his eyes. Serenity was stepping into the tub. *What a sight! The woman is beautiful.* He still couldn't believe his fortune. She was what most men dream about—and she was ready to take a bath with him.

If this is a dream, I will kill anyone who wakes me up.

Chapter Twenty-Nine

SERENITY SLID DOWN INTO THE tub and faced Omar.

He groaned, and said, "Angel, you are killing me. Right now, my willpower is waning. If we continue to sit like this, I am going to bury myself so deep inside of you that both of us will start screaming. I don't want to have any regrets later. Please turn around."

She reached for the iPod on the counter, hit a button, and played "Let Me Be Your Angel" by Jennifer Hudson. She reached behind her for his erect penis and asked, "Is this for me?"

He replied, "Only for you, my angel." He took one of her breasts in his hand and placed two fingers of his other hand in her vagina.

They listened to the song while making love with their hands and mouths. She came moments before the song ended, and his release came with the last note of the song.

When he could speak, he told her he loved her. He asked her to give them a chance because their crazy schedules were only temporary—and he knew in his heart that what they had between them was permanent.

She looked at him with wonder in her eyes.

He told her that he knew she cared for him—and might even love him.

When she opened her mouth to speak, he placed a finger over her mouth and said, "Don't say anything. I can see it in your eyes and feel it when you touch me. When you are ready, you will say it."

They got out of the tub, had a late dinner in bed, and went back to discovering each other with their hands and mouths until they fell asleep.

Serenity woke up at three and couldn't go back to sleep. She knew it was nine in New York. She went into her office and called Trish. When Trish answered, Serenity said, "I'm in big trouble."

Trish was shocked to hear cool, calm, and collected Serenity sounding like she was having a panic attack. Trish told Serenity to breathe in through her nose and exhale through her mouth. They did the breathing exercise until Serenity told Trish that she was feeling better

Trish asked Serenity what had gotten her so upset and what kind of trouble was she in, and Serenity told her everything.

Trish started laughing and said, "A drop-dead gorgeous man who is successful, smart, has the telephone numbers for most of the movers and shakers of the world flew across the world to be with you and told you he loves you—and you think you are in trouble?"

"Yes."

"Why are you afraid?"

"Because I love him. I couldn't tell him, but he knows. I always thought that when I fell in love, I would have the time to devote to the relationship. I can't even find the time to get a few weeks off. How can I be in a relationship with someone when I can't find the time to be in same zip code with him for more than a weekend? What if the tabloids find out about us? I want the type of relationship our parents have."

Trish told her she would have that kind of relationship when the time was right. They would deal with the tabloids when they had to. "You need to live in the moment and enjoy whatever time you can get with your gorgeous man."

Serenity thanked Trish for the advice, but she was still scared.

"Stop analyzing the situation. Listen to your heart. When the time is right, you'll tell Omar that you love him."

Chapter Thirty

When Serenity returned to bed, Omar was awake.

He said, "I reached out for you, and you were gone. I thought you ran out on me in the middle of the night."

She gave a nervous laugh and said, "Why would I run away from my home?"

"Come here. To survive in my line of work, I have to know how to read people. Their eyes, body language, breathing patterns, and overall behavior tell me what I need to know about them. Couple my training with my connection with you—and I can read you like a book.

"When I told you I loved you, you freaked. You couldn't sleep, so you called a close confidante to seek help. I don't know what they told you to help calm you down. You are still not completely calm. I wouldn't be surprised if you ran away in the middle of the night and left me in your home."

She looked at him and said, "Remind me not to play poker with you. I'm scared because this relationship thing is new to me. We have known each other less than a New York minute and the L-word was put out there. I run my life on a schedule—and love is not on the schedule for another couple of years. I will have to regroup because I want you in my life. I don't know what to do. Slow down and give me some time. At the rate you're going, you will have us married with 2.5 children by next week."

He doubled over laughing. When he could talk, he told her she had forgotten to mention the dog. Omar said, "Take all the time you need for your brain to catch up with your heart." He gave her a passionate kiss and said, "Let's get some sleep."

Chapter Thirty-One

THEY SPENT A GLORIOUS WEEK in Madrid. Omar visited his Madrid office for a couple of hours a few days, and then he spent the remainder of his time doing what he came to Madrid to do—spending time with his angel.

He acclimated himself to Serenity's group and saw a glimmer of one part of her world. It wasn't as glamorous as they made it look on TV and in the magazines. At nights, he pampered her. They had toe-curling sex and got to know each other.

On Saturday, they flew back to New York. They discussed his schedule for June.

Omar was leaving on Sunday for Germany, but he would be back on the Thursday before the wedding. He let her know that texting was the best way to communicate with him.

Serenity and Omar sat in each other's arms and explored each other. At one point, she realized that Omar had removed her bra and was fondling her bare breast under her blouse.

He started sucking her nipples without removing her blouse, and it was driving her crazy. She pulled his shirt from his jeans and moved her hands up his chest; she made small circles around his nipples and pulling on them.

They both were getting turned on. She then unzipped his jeans, put her hand in his boxers, and started stroking his penis. Their moaning started to become too loud, so they decided to take the action into the bedroom.

In the bedroom, they took their time stripping each other, kissing and licking the areas where a piece of clothing was removed. Serenity finished stripping Omar first and took the lead by kissing and licking him all over his body. She got down on her knees and began licking and sucking Omar's erection.

When he couldn't take any more of the sweet pleasures she was giving him, he lifted her up, placed her on the bed, and entered her. Omar brought Serenity close to her release several times; he would pull out and start over again until she begged for her release.

They finally found the release they were seeking, and Omar covered Serenity's mouth with his to stifle their screams.

When they regained their ability to speak, he said, "We are now official members of the Mile High Club. Another first for me."

They took a shower, got dressed, and slept until it was time to return to their seats for landing.

When they arrived in New York, they went to Serenity's home. Omar stayed with her and left around five.

Before leaving, Omar stood at the open door. He thought she looked just like a sleeping angel.

Chapter Thirty-Two

WHEN SERENITY WOKE UP, SHE looked for Omar in her bed. She realized that she would not be with him for almost a month—and admitted that she loved him. She was afraid to let him know.

She missed the way he made her feel when she was with him. Her phone started to play "Angel" by Jennifer Hudson and she knew it was Omar.

He wanted to hear her voice before he left. He reminded her that he might not have time for actual phone calls, but he would text her as often as possible. He asked what time her doctor's appointment was and if she would be leaving for California after the appointment.

She told him her appointment was at eleven o'clock, and she would be leaving for LA at three. They talked for a while, and then told each other to have safe trips and they would miss each other.

Serenity thought, *And now it begins. This is the beginning of our long-distance relationship. For the next four months, we will see each for only one weekend, and some of that time will be spent with others at a wedding. Is this any way to begin a relationship? Maybe I should end it before we are too vested in a relationship that might not work out due to the lack of proximity. And honestly, do I need a man to complicate my life?*

I told my parents and Trish that we are a couple, and I know that I love him. Deep down, I don't think I am ready for a committed relationship. The sex is fantastic. He is a caring man, and he shows me that he loves me when he is around. He makes me laugh, and we have fun together. I am not ready for my love life to be splattered across the tabloids and analyzed by the entertainment shows. Right now, I am flying under the paparazzi radar, but it won't be that way for long. When they find out about Omar, the frenzy will begin. I don't think I am ready for that. Is Omar ready for his life to be disrupted and scrutinized?

Serenity had more questions than answers. Since they both would be traveling, it might be all right not to make a decision right then, but the time would come when she had to decide what to do about their so-called relationship.

Serenity called Mama B and explained everything.

Mama B said, "If you love this man like you say you do, when you are ready to settle down with him, nothing will stand in your way. All the obstacles and barriers you are putting up now will crumble when you are ready. Just give it time."

After speaking with Mama B, Serenity felt better. She went into the bathroom to get ready for her appointment.

Chapter Thirty-Three

AFTER LANDING IN FRANKFURT, GERMANY, and checking into his hotel, Omar texted Serenity to give her his hotel information and ask about her appointment and her trip.

When she got to her townhouse, Serenity read Omar's text. She texted him back to let him know that she was officially on birth control. When he got home, he would not need to wear his gloves when they had sex. Her trip to Los Angeles was uneventful. The media circus—or "dog-and-pony show" as her grandmother called it—would start at the film premiere.

She would do the American tour for a week and leave for London on Saturday. The London premiere would be on Sunday. Trish would be with her for the duration, and that was the only benefit of the trip. She told him she loved making movies, but she hated promoting them

Omar asked her to let him know what hotel she would be staying at in London. He was sorry that he couldn't be with her, but he was glad that Trish would be there.

Serenity put on her swimsuit and went out to the pool. Swimming was the only exercise she liked; it relaxed her. She had a very high metabolism and burned up calories quickly. She also ate a healthy diet. If she had to torture herself by exercising for hours and only eating vegetables and drinking mineral water, running Sanders Industries would be her only job. After her swim, she took a shower and had a grilled salmon salad with ginger dressing for dinner.

Trish loved California, and Los Angeles was her home base. Serenity was thankful that they could afford to travel to see each other whenever they needed to.

Trish was going to the Viper Room with Den. She asked Serenity if she wanted to go with them. Serenity told her thanks, but no thanks. She was going stay in, listen to her iPod, and read the new scripts her agent had waiting for her when she arrived at the townhouse.

Trish said, "You sound down. What's bothering you?"

"Starting tomorrow, we will be together for the next month. We can talk during that time."

"Do you need company?"

"Go enjoy your night on the town with Den. The Viper Room is where you'll start—but that's not where the night will end."

"You know me too well."

After she got off the phone, serenity's doorbell rang. A delivery person handed her the most beautiful arrangement of tropical flowers she had ever seen. She tipped the delivery person, closed the door, and read the card to see who had sent the arrangement. Of course, it was Omar.

She put them in her bedroom because she wanted them to be the last thing she saw before she went to sleep—and the first thing she saw in the morning.

Chapter Thirty-Four

THE FILM PREMIERE WAS VERY successful. The movie studio suggested that Serenity and the male lead should go together and act like they were a couple because this could create more publicity for the movie. They had known each other since she was sixteen and he was nineteen.

They had worked on other projects together, and they got along well. He would have been the brother she wished for. The studio was not aware that he was gay. He had been in a committed relationship with his partner for three years. Acting like they were a couple would not be a problem for them. She wondered if it would be an issue for Omar. Oh well! It was one more thing she would have to add to the list.

When Serenity got home, her phone rang.

Omar said, "Hi, angel. How was the premiere? And did you have fun at the parties."

"Based on the premiere, I think the film will be a success. I did have fun at the after-parties. Trish, Den, and the male lead in the film never left my side."

After thanking him for the beautiful floral arrangement, she told him he would be seeing pictures of her and the male lead actor looking like they were in love, but it was only for publicity. She explained to him the actor's relationship status.

Omar said, "Angel, I trust you. When you give me a reason to be jealous, then we will talk about it. Thank you for the advance notice about the pictures and your date for the premiere."

She asked about his meetings, and he told her that he didn't know because all he could think about in the meetings was making love to her. She told him he might have to give his clients a refund because they were not getting their money's worth if he was thinking about making love when he should be concentrating on business.

Omar laughed and told her his second-in-command was taking a lot of notes, so it would be okay. They talked some more, and he told her to get some rest.

The next day's papers showed that audiences and film critics had given the film excellent reviews. They raved about the performances of the lead actors.

That week, she went on several talk shows to promote the film. Before her plane left for London, Serenity texted her hotel information to Omar.

Den would be traveling with Serenity and Trish. He would stay with them for the London premiere and then travel with them to Italy. Because Den was with them, Serenity never got a chance to talk with Trish about her fears of committing to Omar. She knew they would have alone time soon and was not worried. She would just enjoy the company.

Chapter Thirty-Five

SERENITY AND OMAR EXCHANGED TEXTS on a daily basis. On Saturday, he told her he would try to call her the next day and wished her a successful premiere.

When Serenity got to her hotel in London, a bouquet of tropical flowers was waiting for her. She knew they were from Omar.

On Sunday, she was tied up with press conferences until the afternoon. She barely had time to eat, take a shower, and get ready for the premiere

After the premiere and parties, she was tired. She checked her phone and didn't see a text or a missed call from Omar. She decided to take a bath and call Trish to find out what time they would be leaving for Italy.

She got out of the tub; she put on her plush bathrobe, and went to make her call. Just as she picked up the phone, there was a knock on her door.

Believing it was room service; she opened the door and said, "You are just in time."

"In time for what, angel?"

Omar was the last person Serenity expected to see, but he was a welcome surprise. She jumped in his arms.

He picked her up, and she kissed him all over his face. He told her that she smelled like a beautiful flower—and he wanted to know what she had on under her bathrobe.

Just as he bent his head down to kiss her and remove her robe, there was another knock at the door. This time it was room service.

Omar tipped the woman and told her to put the tray on the table.

"Serenity, what do you want first—me or the food?"

She said, "I want you."

Chapter Thirty-Six

O MAR REMOVED SERENITY'S BATHROBE AND got his answer. She was naked under her robe. He knelt in front of her, took her in his arms, and started sucking and licking her everywhere. He traveled the full length of her body, making love to her with his mouth and hands.

Omar's actions elicited moans and gyrations from Serenity. She begged him for her release.

He moved down her body once more and settled between her legs. He opened her lower lips and used his tongue—and then his fingers—to get her juices flowing.

Serenity had never experienced this type of sensation and was scared of what she was feeling. She dug her fingers into the sofa cushions as her world spiraled out of control.

Omar continued to lick and rub her sensitive spot until she had an orgasm that left her breathless. He moved back up her body, leaving kisses everywhere. He rubbed her back and massaged her shoulders until she was able to breathe normally again.

Serenity had never felt so relaxed.

Omar took her to the bedroom, undressed, and got into bed with her. They cuddled and went to sleep. He awoke to Serenity massaging his penis.

She asked what he wanted her to do to please him. He told her to keep doing what she was doing. Serenity used her hands and mouth to pleasure Omar until he was on the brink of an orgasm.

He pulled her up and told her to get on top. She rode him, and he plunged deeper and deeper into her. Just as she was on the verge of an orgasm, he flipped her over and got on top of her. He pulled out of her and then went back in deeper. He did this until she climaxed, and he followed moments later. They lay on the bed, gasping for air.

Serenity said, "I have read about mind-blowing sex, and now I have experienced it." She reached over and kissed him.

Omar and Serenity made love, woke up, and made love some more. In the early morning, they fell asleep.

They woke around nine and ordered room service. Just as they were about to get in the shower, Trish knocked on the door.

Trish walked in the suite, and said, "You lost your phone again—didn't you? I tried calling you, and it went straight to voice mail. I texted and didn't get a reply. I called your suite directly and didn't get an answer. Your bodyguards told me that you haven't left your suite. So I came to see if your boyfriend sent his men to abduct you from the hotel."

Serenity laughed and said, "No, he didn't send anyone. He came himself. We turned our phones off and unplugged the landline."

Trish said, "It's about time you experienced a wild night of sex. Is two o'clock all right for us to leave for Venice?"

They agreed on the time, and Trish left the suite with a smile on her face.

Chapter Thirty-Seven

A FTER BREAKFAST, OMAR ASKED SERENITY about her plans for the day.

She was going to hang out in her suite and play cards with her bodyguard or read until it was time to leave for Venice.

He asked if she wanted to take a stroll around Hyde Park.

She told him that she couldn't; she was not ready to make their relationship public. The publicity tour for the film had created a media frenzy. Their relationship made her feel normal; the moment the media got a hold of it, she would lose the normalcy.

He looked at her, shook his head, and gave her a hug.

The London movie premiere was a success. In Venice, Serenity and Trish stayed with Den at his villa on the water. Den's security team worked with Serenity's security team, and they afforded Serenity and Trish more freedom to move around. They spent three days in Venice and then left for Paris.

On the plane to Paris, Trish said to Serenity, "I am glad to see that Omar is scheduling time to be with you."

Serenity told Trish that, in addition to Omar telling her that he loves her, he treats her like an angel—and the sex is fantastic.

Trish said, "I hear a 'but' in there someplace."

Serenity said, "Because of my film and modeling careers, I can't bring myself to tell him that I love him. Now is not the right time for us. When we were in London, he wanted us to take a stroll in Hyde Park, but I turned him down."

"What did Omar say?"

"He looked at me and shook his head."

"Are you in love with Omar? Do you see a future with him? If you can answer yes to those two questions, you will find a way to make the relationship works. You are afraid of going into a relationship because you think you will lose control of your life. In a good relationship, partners help and nurture each other; they don't control each other."

"When did you become so knowledgeable about relationships?"

"I had to kiss a lot of frogs. Based on our parents' example of good relationships, I knew what I was looking for. Omar is not a millionaire playboy. He loves you. Together, both of you are more outgoing. He anticipates your needs and fulfills them. If I were choosing a man for you, it would be Omar."

Serenity thanked Trish for listening. She asked Trish how it was going with Den.

Trish told her they were in a committed relationship, and it would result in marriage in six months to a year.

Serenity reminded Trish of their promise to plan each other's weddings.

When they arrived at their hotel in Paris, Serenity and Trish had floral bouquets waiting for them from their men. They went to their suites and made phone calls. They were staying at a five-star hotel near the Eiffel Tower and Notre Dame Cathedral. That night after the film's premiere, Serenity went back to the hotel and called Omar.

She thanked him for the flowers and told him that the view from her hotel was out of this world.

He told her he had stayed at the hotel a couple of times.

She told him she wished he was there to share the view with her.

He said, "Maybe one day we can return together and enjoy the city of love and lights."

She said, "That sounds good."

Chapter Thirty-Eight

T HE PREMIERE WENT WELL IN Barcelona.

On their way to Berlin, Serenity told Trish that she could remember when traveling around the world was exciting. Now all she could think about was returning home and sleeping in her own bed. She needed a vacation to relax and think. Would it matter if she achieved fame and fortune but she didn't have a life?

She let Trish in on her plans to start phasing out her film and modeling responsibilities. By the time she was twenty-eight, she would be retired from modeling. She would do a movie now and then, but her primary focus would be Sanders Industries.

"Does your decision have anything to do with Omar?"

"No. This is a decision I made about a year ago, and I am just starting to verbalize it."

Serenity and Trish continued to have flowers waiting for them at their hotels. Serenity and Omar continued to communicate with calls or texts.

The last leg of their trip was the longest. After the Berlin premiere, Serenity had several radio, TV, and magazine interviews. The next day, Omar texted her to let her know that he was back in New York and was looking forward to seeing her.

Serenity called Omar and they talked about everything. She told him she would be back in New York the day before the wedding. She asked if he had let his friend know that he was bringing a date to the wedding. He had forgotten to call but would do it the next day. She told him she had a secret plan for how to go unnoticed at the wedding.

Three days later, Serenity and Trish landed in New York. Den was back in New York, and Trish would be staying with him.

When Serenity got to her penthouse, she texted Omar to let him know she was home. He called her immediately, welcomed her home, and invited her to have lunch with him at his home later that day.

She asked where and when the wedding would be. He told her the ceremony would take place at St. Patrick's Cathedral at five o'clock—and the reception would be at the Plaza Hotel.

She yawned, told him she would see him later, and ended the call.

Chapter Thirty-Nine

O MAR OPENED HIS EYES AND looked at the alarm clock on the bedside table. It was six o'clock. He got up and took a shower. In the shower, his mind drifted to the one person who took up space in his thoughts. He knew that Serenity cared for him and was always glad to see him. However, sometimes he felt like he was the one who wanted the relationship. Serenity appeared to want a friend with benefits.

After the wedding, he would have a serious discussion with Serenity to determine what she wanted out of the relationship. He was looking for a wife and the future mother of his kids. He could see Serenity in that role, but he needed to know if it was a role she was willing to take on. He sounded like a damn movie producer. What was he going to do—talk her into taking on the lifetime role of becoming his wife? He loved her, wanted her, and didn't think he could live without her, but he refused to beg her to love him.

He would be thirty-one in November, and he wanted to start his family when he was in his thirties. He didn't want to be one of those old farts who couldn't keep up with his kids. He wanted to be able to take his kids on hikes, ride bikes, and play ball without anyone having to call the paramedics. Little kids have a lot of energy, and they should have parents that can keep up with them at least 80 percent of the time. His father was still young enough to play basketball and go golfing with him; he wanted that with his kids.

Omar called his father to shoot the breeze. It still amazed him that his father always sounded genuinely happy to hear from him. They discussed his most recent trip and his upcoming three-month trip.

"With all the traveling you are doing, do you have time to romance Serenity?"

"I'm working on it, but the lady in question seems to be stuck in neutral"

"Son, you are very spontaneous. When you get an idea, you act on it immediately. Serenity is very cautious—who can blame her? In her line of work, she is surrounded by people who make a living by pretending."

I'll back off for a while. But if Serenity doesn't shift out of neutral, I'll take over the driver's seat."

Please don't kidnap her and take her to some cave in the Middle East where we won't be able to find you."

"I can't make any promises, but I love you."

Chapter Forty

SERENITY WOKE UP WITH A headache and cramps. All she wanted to do was stay in bed for the next few years until she could make a decision about Omar. She wondered how long she had before he forced her to make their relationship public. She could tell by the look in his eyes when he offered to take her for a stroll in Hyde Park that he was holding back his anger with her. *Why the hell did he have to show up in my life now? Couldn't he have waited a couple of years? That's Omar for you. He only knows one speed—and it is fast!*

Mrs. Pen was glad to have Serenity home. She fussed over her and thanked Serenity for the new Lladro figurine. Due to Serenity's generosity, Mrs. Pen had a very large Lladro collection.

Serenity kissed Mrs. Penn on the cheek and said, "I remember visiting you when I was eight years old. I saw that beautiful figurine on your dresser, and you allowed me to play with it. When I got older, I realized that you allowed an eight-year-old to play with something that was of value in sentiment and had monetary value attached to it. I knew I had to help you start a collection."

Mrs. Pen hugged Serenity and said, "You are the granddaughter I never had."

Serenity went in her bathroom, turned on the tap, poured in her favorite bath salts, and turned on the Jacuzzi. She removed Omar's T-shirt and slid into the tub. His T-shirts had become her permanent sleeping attire when he was not around.

When he is around, I sleep in his arms butt naked. If anyone had told me that I would enjoy sleeping in my birthday suit, I wouldn't have believed it. Omar is pulling me out of my shell sexually—and in other areas of my life. Am I in love with Omar—or do I just love being with him? My heart tells me I am in love with him—and to jump into the relationship with both feet. My head is telling me to be cautious and take my time. What the hell is wrong with me? I make business decisions involving millions of dollars without blinking. Why can't I make a decision about a man?

A knock on the bathroom door brought Serenity out of her musings. Mrs. Pen was the only other person in the house. She said, "Come in, Mrs. Pen."

Mrs. Pen poked her head around the door and asked if Serenity was okay.

"Thanks for checking on me. I'll be out soon."

She got out of the tub, dressed, and told Mrs. Pen she was meeting Omar for lunch.

Chapter Forty-One

WHEN SERENITY ARRIVED AT OMAR'S penthouse, the guard said, "Welcome home, Ms. Sanders."

She smile at him and said, thank you."

When she got off the elevator in Omar's apartment, he greeted her with a big bear hug. He lifted her up and walked her to the den. She was giggling and telling him to put her down.

"I don't think I can let you go."

They hugged and kissed on the couch until his housekeeper came and got them for lunch.

Lunch consisted of grilled tuna, brown rice, spring salad with ginger-lime dressing, and pineapple lemonade. On the side, there was homemade angel's food cake with strawberries and a buttercream sauce.

"Are you close with the groom?"

"We get together whenever we can. I was asked to be in the wedding party, but I turned it down because of my travels. When we were in college, Frank had a different girlfriend every week, and he ran around with a wild bunch of boys and girls. Now Frank is a respected world-renowned civil rights attorney, and he's marrying the love of his life."

He asked about her earlier years, her friendship with Trish, and how she went into modeling and films at fifteen.

"Trish traveled with me. Three teachers traveled with us until we graduated from high school."

"Did Trish's parents have any objections to her traveling with you?"

"Both our parents are doctors with only daughters they adore. Trish demonstrated excellent negotiation skills from a young age."

"How about college?"

"I had fun in Boston. College was great because I was allowed more freedom to enjoy my time away at school."

"Would you like to go back to Paris in November to celebrate our birthdays?"

She hesitated, took some time to think about it, and agreed.

Because Serenity was seeing her period, they spent the afternoon getting to know more about each other, and sleeping in each other's arms without making love.

At 2:30, Serenity went home to get dressed for the wedding.

Chapter Forty-Two

MRS. PEN GREETED OMAR WHEN he got off the elevator and offered him a drink. He requested water.

Omar was flipping through an album when a gorgeous woman with shoulder-length midnight-black hair and blue eyes appeared at the door. She was dressed in a peach, Grecian-style gown with a diamond broach on her left shoulder. The outfit was finished off with nude Jimmy Choo peep-toe stilettos and matching clutch.

Serenity said, "Do I look that different? If your answer is yes, then I have achieved the effect I was going for. I want tonight to be about your friend and his bride."

Omar said, "Come here. Let me hold you to make sure my angel is under there."

He took her in his arms, molded his body to hers, and said, "Yes, you are in there."

"Tonight my name is Angel Snow."

He bent over laughing and said, "So tonight you are my snow angel?"

She smiled and said, "Yes, I am."

When he let her go, Serenity stepped back and looked at Omar. *This man is more handsome than moist of the models and leading men I have worked with.*

Omar said, "Am I overdressed? I thought a tux was appropriate for a formal wedding."

"You are gorgeous. If you want to moonlight as an actor or a model, I could get you some gigs."

"Thank you for the compliment. I am yours alone."

At the wedding, Serenity was introduced to the bride and groom and their parents. They mingled, socialized, and had fun with the other guests. Because of their innate shyness, they only left each other when they had to go to the restroom.

Twice Serenity was asked to dance with relatives of the bride and groom. Both times she could tell by the look in Omar's eyes and the clench of his jaw that he didn't want her dancing with anyone else. For the remainder of the evening, Omar was her only dance partner.

While Serenity was in the restroom, Frank and Dana took Omar aside.

Frank said, "When did you become a playboy?"

Omar said, "What are you talking about?"

Frank said, "My mom told me that your mom told her you were dating Serenity Sanders—and then you appear at my wedding with another beautiful woman."

Omar smiled and whispered, "This is for your ears only. Angel Snow and Serenity Sanders are the same person. She didn't want the paparazzi disrupting your wedding—so she came as Angel Snow."

Dana said, "Whoever she is—she is the most beautiful woman I have ever seen."

Frank looked at his bride and said, "To me, you are the most beautiful woman I have ever seen."

Chapter Forty-Three

O N THE LIMO RIDE HOME, Serenity said, "Thanks for inviting me. I had a wonderful time."

"It was wonderful for me too. The only low point of the evening was when those two goons were holding you too close while you were dancing with them."

She kissed him and said, "You are the only one I want."

He kissed her back, and the conversation ended.

When they got to her apartment, Serenity said she was going to change clothes and would be back in a moment. She returned in one of his T-shirts, black leggings, no makeup, and her hair was braided down her back. She took his breath way because she looked more gorgeous than when she was dressed up.

She sat next to him on the sofa, and he took her in his arms.

He asked, "When can we make love again?"

"Next Friday."

"Damn! I am leaving on Monday morning for my three-month trip. I can't wait that long to be inside of you. I want you now!"

Serenity took Omar to her bedroom and used her hands and mouth to give him some relief.

The next day, Serenity donned her Angel Snow wig and contacts, and they went sailing on the Hudson River. The day was relaxing, and they both felt great.

They went to Serenity's apartment. Omar used condoms, and they made love several times during the afternoon.

They were relaxing on the sofa with Serenity's head on Omar's chest while he massaged her scalp.

Omar lifted her head up and said, "This will be my last extended trip. I have made some changes in my schedule so I will be home more. I have a question to ask you. When I return in September, I will ask the question again. I will expect your answer then. For now, I just want you to think about it."

"What's the question?"

Omar looked her in the eyes and said, "I want to spend the rest of my life with you. I want you to be the mother of my children. Will you marry me?"

Serenity looked at Omar and said, "I would have to say no!"

"I asked you to think about it and give me your answer in three months."

"Nothing will change in three months. My life will still be complicated."

"I can help you uncomplicate your life."

"It wasn't complicated until I decided to enter a relationship with you." She got up to get a drink of water, and Omar waited. She came back to the sofa and said, "I don't like complications in my personal life. I like what we have now. Why do you want to change it?"

Chapter Forty-Four

OMAR MOVED A CHAIR IN front of Serenity, sat down, looked into her eyes, and said, "I want you to listen to what I am about to say to you because this might be the most important discussion I will ever have with you. I will give you three months to decide if you want to be my wife. I refuse to be the boy toy you keep hidden away in New York. Loving someone means taking a chance. When you fall in love, you are opening up yourself to rejection, loss, and many other possibilities.

"It is a chance worth taking if you end up with the one person in the world you want to spend the rest of your life with. I am willing to take a chance with you. You have to ask yourself if this man sitting in front of you is worth loving and taking a chance with. Only you can answer that question.

"I love you with my heart and soul. I would do anything for you, but I will not beg you for your love. You will have to give me your love freely. I will be back the first week in September. You have until then to decide if you want to be my wife. When I leave here tonight, I will not call, text, Skype, or e-mail you.

I will back off and leave you alone so you can go back to your uncomplicated life."

Omar kissed Serenity passionately and walked to the elevator. When the elevator came, he got on and looked at Serenity until the doors closed.

Serenity could not move; she felt dazed and confused.

Coming soon, look for **I Give You My Love Freely**. Did Serenity decide that Omar was worth the risk?

Excerpt:

Serenity hugged herself and started rocking. She asked herself, "What just happen? What did I do?" She started crying and rocking back and forth.

She needed to talk with someone. She can't call her mom or her grandmother—and upset them. Omar won't pick up if she calls him. Where is Trish? Just as she was about to call Trish her phone rang with Trish's ring tone. She said, "I need you," drop the phone—and started crying uncontrollably.

Trish kept on calling Serenity's name in the phone but all she could hear was Serenity crying. She knew it was serious. Her sister is not a drama queen something must be gravely wrong for her to be crying like this.

Trish couldn't wait for her driver to get to Den's apartment. She calls down to security and asked them to have a taxi waiting for her when she gets down stairs. She throws some clothes in an overnight bag, told Den Serenity needed her, kisses him—and left the apartment.

Trish got into the waiting taxi, gave the driver her destination and told him if he gets her there in ten minutes she will give him two hundred dollars. The driver got her there in seven minutes.

When Trish got off the elevator in Serenity's apartment the place was in darkness and she heard a sound coming from the master bedroom that sounded like—nothing she had ever heard before—or wanted to hear again.

She went into the bedroom; to prevent from flooding the room with light, she turned on the light in the sitting area. She saw Serenity lying on the bed in the fetal position rocking and making that sound that she can't describe.

Trish was not ready to know what made the normally calm and composed person that lived up to the name of serenity so frazzled. She took Serenity in her arms held her like a baby, and sang to her until she fell asleep.

Trish wondered if Serenity and Omar had a fight. She wanted to call Omar and asked him what the hell he did to her sister. Serenity is usually the one talking Trish off the ledge after a break up. *What did he do to her; I am going to kick his handsome ass.*